ALS

MW01119048

KIMBERLY'S CLIENTS SERIES
The Hunting Lease

FARMERS' STEPDAUGHTERS SERIES
Darla
Tiffany
Nissa

SHERIFF BILL SERIES
First Time with Sheriff Daddy
Virgin Butt Ranch
Getting Some Posse

STAND ALONE BOOKS
Cheerleader Butt Squad
Expectant
Uberdaddy
Naughty Bookstore Girls

ALSO FROM QUICKIE PRESS
Sexchanger by E.B. Schechter

Pass Me around the Locker Room

By Jennifer Grey

It was good to be back in college. Kimberly's boss, Willie Wiel, had picked up some clients that were very well-heeled, and that meant more work for her. After a year of making the rounds, she had just enough for her first semester tuition. But the bills were coming due for the spring semester and she needed a big paycheck. There's no shortage of demand for a fine piece of tail, and Kimberly definitely had that reputation, so Willie came back pretty quick with an opportunity. He had known a particular alumnus of the college for a while. An electric car tycoon, the man had contributed millions to the football program and could pretty much do whatever and get whatever he wanted at the university.

Kimberly checked her look in the full-length mirror of her dormitory room. Not that the football players she was about to service would be too particular, but she did have her reputation to think of. Looking cute is good business. And she was sooo cute, from her delicate, straight blond hair, to her small, firm breasts, to her shapely belly and legs, to her smooth pussy. Turning around and looking over her shoulder, she admired her small, firm, sexy ass. She caressed her smooth skin wondering exactly how that ass would be used that night.

Mr. Biggs showed up in his limousine, and his driver held the door as Kimberly crawled into the enormous leather-lined back seat. He had a big smile and a mouth full of teeth. He wore a Brioni suit that probably cost more than her next year of college. She'd learned to recognize the brand, and other such accoutrements of the rich in the past year. In his left hand Biggs held an unlit cigar. The right hand held out a drink for Kimberly. Whiskey. Her favorite pain-killer.

"Well don't you look nice," he said with a Texas drawl. She smiled and winked at him. She was wearing her tightest, whitest tights. From the waist down she looked as if she was naked with white paint covering her body. She wore a tight crop top and no bra – her tits were so small and firm that she didn't need one. "I believe you're the cutest little thing I've ever seen," he said.

"You want to fuck me big daddy?" she teased. But she knew that might be part of the deal.

"Goodness no, child! I'm a married man." Kimberly raised her eyebrows, but said nothing and just looked out the window. After a pause, he said, "No, I'm afraid all I'm allowed is a blow job." Kimberly laughed, a little too loudly, and crawled over to him. She snuggled in and ran her hand up his leg, enjoying the feel of expensive wool. She'd come to like older, wealthy men as much as younger men. They knew what they wanted. Even the smell of cigar smoke and whiskey made her feel at home. Her hand had reached his crotch and found his cock. She was already having an effect, and she felt him growing under the luxurious cloth. In a minute she was kneeling in front of him unwrapping his goods.

Mr. Biggs was accustomed to getting what he wanted, and he was not disappointed with the product Willie Wiel had sent him. Her hands were like steel vices lined with silk. As she gripped him with one hand she ran her other hand over the oxford shirt covering his chest. Her mouth was on fire. Mr. Biggs had been around and had many young girls suck his cock, but he'd never experienced a performance like what this blonde nymph was putting on. She felt him twitching and grabbed his balls and squeezed gently but firmly as he released his come into her throat. Kimberly swallowed with him growing soft in her mouth. Then she looked up at his face with a sweet grin. He was beaming from ear to ear.

Mr. Biggs zipped up and Kimberly arranged her hair.

"Sweetie," he said, putting his arm around her, "that's the best I've ever had, and I mean it." He handed her five hundred-dollar bills. "You earned that." The car had stopped. The door opened and they got out. "You treat my boys real nice tonight and there will be more." He started walking toward the elevator to the sky boxes. "Eric will take you where you need to go." The limo driver, Eric, nodded to her and led her past security guards and down a staircase to a tunnel. There they sat in a golf cart and watched the game on a television attached to the wall. When it was over, Eric stood up.

"Be ready for a ride," he said.

"I'm always ready for a ride," Kimberly replied wryly.

"No," said Eric. "I'm serious. They're going to grab you on the way in."

Kimberly pondered this, but thought, "What the hell?" I'm in for something tonight and it won't be tame.

The team ran off the field and into the tunnel. The first players to come in saw Eric and their faces lit up. Apparently this was not a one-time thing. They were obviously used to "gifts" from alumni. A large, sweaty African-American player walked straight up to her and said "Hi! I'm Rodney, but everybody calls me The Rod." He put his hands on her waist and threw her over his shoulder effortlessly, like she was an overcoat. Then The Rod started whooping and yelling and they marched down the tunnel.

Kimberly saw nothing but The Rod's number upside down on his journey, until they were going over red carpet. They had arrived in the locker room. The Rod took her to the back row of lockers and laid her down on a narrow bench. She was covered in his sweat. By the time she looked up at him he already had his jersey and shoulder pads off, and was peeling off his pants. Kimberly was already behind. She reached a hand down her pants and found her clit. He wasn't going to wait and she needed to be wet. With her other hand she pulled off her tights. She wore nothing underneath.

The Rod was completely naked before her. His body was a work of art. Rippled abs and sculpted arms, and his legs were like tree trunks. Her eyes were drawn to his sizeable cock, which was rock hard and ready for action. The wetness came quickly. She threw off her shirt and looked him right in the eyes. "Fuck me, Rod! I want that big, black dick in my little white pussy." Before she knew it he was inside her and thrusting like a crazy man. He filled her up and she felt him bottoming out with each stroke. Kimberly could barely get her legs around the big man and dug her heels into his ass. It felt like two steel-belted tires. His sweat dripped on her as he pounded her strained pussy. "God, your cock is so big," she exclaimed.

Kimberly breathlessly held on to that skinny bench for dear life. The Rod was going faster and faster and grunting, eyes closed, thinking of nothing but getting her pussy and making himself come. When he exploded inside her, he rammed his cock in her cunt, pushing her back and almost off the bench. He immediately pulled his dripping dick out of her, smiled, and turned and walked away. The Rod was done for the night, but Kimberly was just getting warmed up. She was horny as hell. Eyes wide, she sat up and looked around for something to grab on to.

Two lean, wiry young hunks stood by their lockers. One was blonde and chiseled, the other had ginger hair and freckles. They were smaller than the other guys, but tall. Kimberly

thought they were probably quarterbacks. They

had been watching the show as they

undressed and now stood there in their

underwear with erections poking out. Still

covered in The Rod's sweat and full of his

come, she dashed to her knees in front of

them, pulled down their boxer briefs, and took

a cock in each hand. She stroked them

lovingly, it seemed, twisting her little hands

around the shafts, applying extra pressure to

their tips with her thumbs on each stroke.

"That feels better," she said with a sigh,

and a smile spread over her face as she

looked up at the two players. Her hair with wet

with her sweat and the steam from the showers

and stuck to her face. Her tits glistened under the harsh fluorescent lights.

"Aren't you going to suck it?" said the blonde player. He had some kind of accent. Kimberly thought it was German or Swedish. The idea of him commanding her was exciting.

"Do you want me to suck it?" she asked seductively.

"Shut up and suck my cock," he said. Just what she wanted to hear. She took him into her mouth, teasing at first, licking the underside of his shaft, all the while moving her hand like a piston up and down the shaft of the redheaded man, who was tensed up, ready to burst. The German was having none of the teasing, and grabbed Kimberly by her hair and forced her onto his cock, now moving his hips, fucking her mouth. The ginger shouted as he came, splashing come on the side of Kimberly's face. She gripped him tightly in her fist as he spasmed and did not let go until she felt him relax. Meanwhile, her other master was getting serious.

"Suck my cock bitch!" She was holding on to the back of his sinewy leg with one hand and constricting his rigid dick with the other. "Suck it! Now take my come and swallow it." The German grunted as he shot his load, still forcing her onto him, until Kimberly dutifully swallowed and he released her.

"Ah, that was good," she said, panting, trying to catch her breath. The German held a hundred-dollar bill to her mouth, she took it from him like a dog taking a biscuit from its master.

Kimberly put the money with her clutch and clothes under the bench where The Rod had fucked her silly. She ran her fingers through her hair and wiped her face with a towel from a clean stack nearby. Now she was ready for some real fun. A wicked smile came over her cute face. She walked to the middle of the room and announced, "I need a cock in my pussy! Who's gonna fuck me next?" There were plenty of guys all around, waiting for a chance at this little hottie that was gifted to them. A big lineman stepped forward. He probably weighed as much as four of her. "Down on the ground," she ordered. The big man grinned and did as he was told, his cock standing at attention, sticking straight up. Kimberly straddled him and guided it between her slick pussy lips, trembling with excitement at what was to come next.

"Now I need a cock in my ass!" she announced once again, now manipulating her hips with the skill of a pro on the lineman's throbbing cock. "No one can multitask like I can," she thought proudly. The next volunteer was approaching. "These guys are so polite not fighting over each other," she thought. Kimberly had taken a small bottle of lubricant from her clutch, and she now spread some lube liberally on her fingers. The man she was fucking was starting to moan and tense up. As she moved her ass up and down, she reached back between her buttocks and sunk two fingers into her anus. It felt good finger-fucking herself in the ass. Her pussy was already sore but her ass was ripe for stimulation. And she wanted to get that going before the big boy in her pussy finished.

A lean, black cornerback moved in behind her. He had a painted-on smile that never seemed to change. Looking over her shoulder at him, she made a pleading face and asked, now timidly, "Would you please fuck me in my ass? I need a dick in my asshole. Please?" He knelt behind her.

"Yeah, baby, I'll fuck that sweet little ass you got." He rubbed the tip of his dick over her pink hole to get it well lubricated, and slid it inside her slowly. "Oh yeah, that's tight. Fuck yeah." Now she was feeling the pressure of two men plunging their cocks into both of her holes at the same time. Waves of euphoria overtook her and she was almost in a trance, letting the two men have her in their own ways. But she wasn't full yet. Sounding a little drunk, she made her final announcement.

Sounding a little drunk, she said "I'm ready to suck a cock. Somebody come fuck me in my mouth. Another hunky player stepped up and put his manhood right in her face. He had been waiting for this. Her hands were on the big man's chest. She gobbled the hunk's half-hard member with her lips. He stiffened as she gave him just a little scrape of her teeth.

She was now completely stuffed and just kept still as three men fucked her in every orifice. She could feel the adrenaline and endorphins coursing through her veins. The players fucking her ass and mouth were jostling her back and forth. As the cornerback thrusted his cock in her ass, he pushed her forward, her mouth coming down on the other man's dick, pushing it all the way into her throat. Her whole body jostled. The big man who had been in her pussy so long was finally tensing up and getting ready to come. He grabbed her little hips with his big hand and tried to control her movement up and down on his cock. She was being pulled in four different directions and loving every second of it.

"I'm gonna come," said the big lineman. She felt his extraordinarily powerful arms forcing her down on him as he twitched inside her. "Aaahhh!" he groaned, so loudly he could have been heard in the skyboxes.

"I'm gonna nut in that booty now," said the black man, speeding up his thrusting, panting furiously. Finally he slammed into her and held on to her hips as he injected semen deep into her.

As the big man wriggled out from under her, and the cornerback pulled his soft cock out of her ass and walked away, Kimberly set her ass down and set herself to finishing off the man in her mouth. She had been unable to do anything with her hands, and now she let them run all over his ass and up to his chest. He started to quiver as his dick received her full attention for the first time. She hungrily, greedily gulped and sucked him, running her tongue all over his shaft. She tightened her lips around him and made him pull almost all the way out of her mouth as she dragged her lips and tongue over his full length. He held on to her head and thrusted rhythmically, faster, in and out of her mouth. She let him do the work. Then he groaned, pulled his cock out from between her lips and splashed his juices all over her flushed face and into her damp hair, rubbing the tip of his dick across her lips as the final spasms completed and his erection subsided.

Kim felt satisfied and just about spent. Most of the players had gone, but there was one young man that did not look like a player. He was wearing jeans and a t-shirt, leaning against the end of a row of lockers. He had been watching as she was gang-banged by three players. She could see a bulge in his jeans. When she looked at him, he looked embarrassed. Kimberly smiled slightly and looked away, collected the hundreds the players had dropped on the floor beside her, and got up to get her things.

As she walked by the man, she asked him, "How old are you?"

"Eighteen," he said. Kimberly wondered who he was. He was staring at her tits. So at least he was normal in that way. Just a kid.

"What's your name?"

"Jason." He thought for a moment, then added, "Jason Biggs." The name rung a bell.

"You want to fuck me in the ass?" She said, smiling. Jason's eyes grew wide. He nodded, then started taking off his clothes. There was no one else in the locker room. "Is this your first time?"

"No, there's been one other time." Kimberly nodded.

"Would you like to put your cock in my ass?" Kimberly got down on her hands and knees and renewed the lubricant in her little pink butthole. It was tender, but not as sore as her pussy was. And it would be a thrill for the second-timer.

"Yes I would," he said. He was now completely naked, knelt behind her. He was young and skinny, but tall. She grabbed some towels to put under her knees so her ass would be high enough for him to enter.

"Well, you should know what to do after the show you just saw. Fuck my ass, big man!" Jason put one hand on her hip and used the other to guide his raging erection into her nether region. He slid it all the way in and thrusted a couple of times.

"Oh!" he exclaimed, jerking involuntarily as he ejaculated. It was all over in a few seconds. He laughed. "Your ass felt so nice and tight."

"Mmm. Thank you!" They stood up and he reached for his wallet. She touched his hand and smiled, kissing him tenderly on the lips.

"This one's on the house, sweetie." She figured he was related to the boss. And if not, well it was a small loss on an hourly basis, anyway.

The next day she got a call from Willie. "I just sent over a bonus from Mr. Biggs. A big one too. You really impressed him."

"Three blowjobs, a hand job, and fucked twice in my ass and twice in my pussy. That should be impressive to anybody.

"Haha. Give me a call next semester. Your price is going up, and there's plenty of demand for your sweet little ass."

"I'm sure we'll talk again."

END OF BOOK TWO

Made in the USA
Las Vegas, NV
28 July 2024

93080316R00018